Nature's Ditties

Lorre Schwepper-Florin

AuthorHouse™
1663 Liberty Drive
Bloomington, IN 47403
www.authorhouse.com
Phone: 1-800-839-8640

First published by AuthorHouse 12/09/2011

ISBN: 978-1-4670-6662-4 (sc)

Library of Congress Control Number: 2011919130

Printed in the United States of America

Any people depicted in stock imagery provided by Thinkstock are models,
and such images are being used for illustrative purposes only.
Certain stock imagery © Thinkstock.

This book is printed on acid-free paper.

Because of the dynamic nature of the Internet, any web addresses or links contained in this book may have changed
since publication and may no longer be valid. The views expressed in this work are solely those of the author and do not
necessarily reflect the views of the publisher, and the publisher hereby disclaims any responsibility for them.

authorHOUSE®

I love my cat And that's a fact. She's all forgiving –
Makes my life worth living. With ear drops And cotton
swabs – with flea spraying and surgical spaying – With
different pills to cure her ills – with stings from vaccine
shots – She loves me lots and lots. With visits to the Vet –
She still considers me her pet.

Lorre Florin

1

I like to visit an old white mare
She trots along to nuzzle my hair
She really sniffs for tasty goodies
She knows I have some oatmeal
Cookies

Graceful dragonfly
Darting in the sky
On transparent wings
Like cellophane things
Looking for a lunch
Of mosquitos by the
bunch
Which do a lot of harm
Biting my tender arm

A snake looks like he
has two tails
With shiny skin
and many scales.
I wonder what
he's really worth—

He's part and
parcel of this earth.

Butterfly flitting to a flower
   Sipping nectar by the hour
      Designs the same on every wing
         He doesn't hurt a living thing
            But, carries pollen all around
               On velvet wings without a sound.

Little squirrel sitting
in a tree
You look so very close
to me
Yet, a spotted window
pane
Separates me from
you and rain
The wind ripples through
your fur
Hey, you're gone!
You're not sitting where
you were

Scurrying across a pebble
To find out what is edible
A big black bug
Tripped over a shiny, slimy slug.
They both went tumbling over
Into a patch of clover.

Poor little Fishy Poo has nothing to do
He sits in his castle — rear fin an axial
With glass on each side and food drifting by — No searching,
No cursing, No hunting, No enemies for bunting. All comforts
provided — nothing decided. He lives in fear
Of boredom, that's clear.

Do you know who
Comes two by two?
There may be twenty
That would be plenty
To eat my lunch—
 munch and munch
That's what they do
Can you
 guess who?

There's a bird hopping on the
branches
All the landscape he enhances
I feed him everyday
Then he flies away.
He thinks it's coming to him—
The food I place upon
the limb.

In his somber winter
coat
He doesn't sing a
thank you note.

Praying mantises are
funny things
Their coat tails are
really wings
Their triangular heads
have big round eyes
That make them look so
very wise
With elbows doubled up
On pesty insects they will sup
Protecting veggies from bad bugs
They deserve our grateful
hugs

I love my cat, for goodness sakes. All my love he surely takes. He's gray and white with wavy tail which swirls around like a billowy sail. If only I could tell him that in the back the mice are fat. There's no need to play with life — to cross the street for a kitty wife. Be safe and sound and stay at home. Forget about the roads to roam.

Fuzzy caterpillar crawling on a
          branch
Aren't you taking an awful
          chance?
A hungry bird can see—
I hope you do believe—
Of you it will devour
You'll be gone
          within the hour

A tortoise is the greatest pet
He's shy and glossy clean
He doesn't live where it is wet
The funniest thing I've ever
                              seen
He looks like a shiny
                  army tank
Or, like a rounded
                  army helmet
Or, a general of the
                  highest rank
With gleaming medals of a set
His back overlaps to form a design
He's brown and geometric
A life of ease — he walks the line
Avoiding what is hectic

14

A bee is very industrious
She isn't very humorous
She's a busy, buzzy
                creature
A fine example of a
                teacher
She works all day
    Doesn't even stop to
                play
She defends her
        homey hive
To keep her family
        all alive

Little mouse sitting on a broom
Soon he'll run to another room
He scampers by the wallboard
Finding crumbs to eat and hoard
When he hears a crashing noise
He stands up tall with regal poise
His back is taunt and straight
And there he'll wail and wait
With senses all alert
Avoiding getting hurt

Spider, spider on the wall
Eight spindly legs in all
Oh, how ugly you are
           to me
But, perfect in such symmetry
Someday I'll understand
Then put you in my
           squeamish hand
And know that all is well
Because you really are our pal.

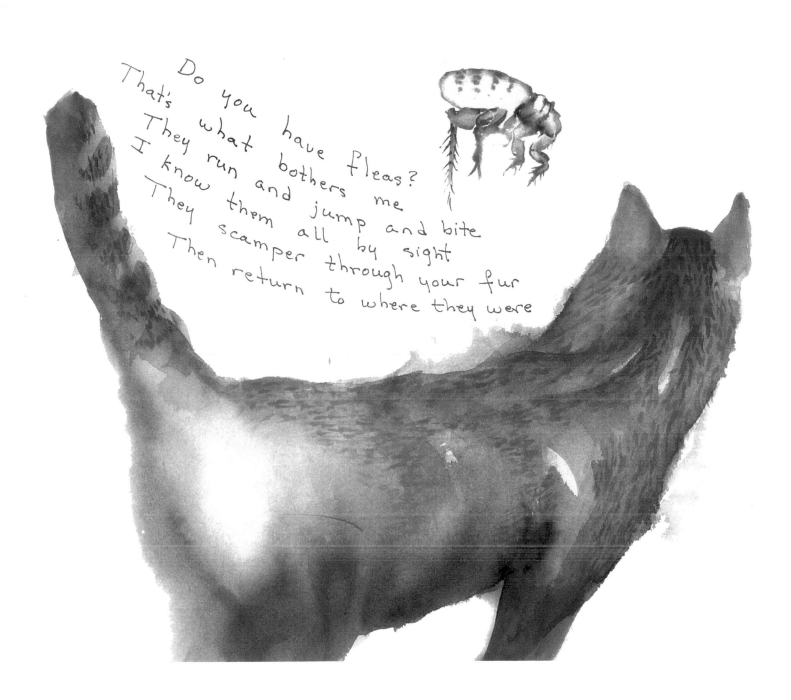

Do you have fleas?
That's what bothers me
They run and jump and bite
I know them all by sight
They scamper through your fur
Then return to where they were

18

Lady Bug sitting on the garden hose
That waters flowers in pretty rows
Is she getting a tasty drink?
Eating aphids, I really think
Her back's so round and
          bright and red
She's very cute, and
          smart, it's said
She's a jewel in
          the yard—
Nature's polka
          dotted
          flower
          guard

Underneath the outside light
A big brown toad comes by night.
I put my finger on his back
Lumps and bumps he doesn't lack
He eats all those flying things
The most delicious are the wings

Little spittle bug
Covered by a frothy foam
How do you get a hug
When in a bubbly home?
No one knows you're there—
Hiding from us all
Camouflaged with special care—
Can you hear us when
        we call?

Lost pet without a home
Busy city streets to roam
Unable to find your way
Are you a lonely stray?
Looking for a family
Trying to live happily
You need someone to care
To groom your matted hair
To feed your empty tummy
With food that's really yummy
To show some warm attention
With a promise of affection

I can't find my cat
How about that!
I call her name just the same
Where could she be?
In that maple tree?
She dozed all day
Now she's gone to play
She'll dine out tonight,
That's her delight,
On bugs and mice—
To her that's nice

Shimmering baby polywog
Wiggling around leaf and log
That float in a muddy pool
In spring when days are cool
Over and under rays of
                        sun
  Head and body
          look like one
Soon tiny legs
        will grow
The web between
        his toes   will show
Then from a tiny polywog
He'll become a slippery frog

There's a puppy at my door
Floppy ears touch the floor
His snout is long
His howl – a song
He'll be my pet
On that I'll bet

The world belongs to
    everything on it
Whether it be ant,
    flea or hornet
Or, whether tree,
    branch or root
Too bad people don't
    give a hoot
All things make a whole
Therefore, take a look
    into your soul

Draw an insect with six legs

Draw a pet you had or wish you had

Draw a spider with eight legs

Write a poem or just some words

Draw something we see in nature around us

CPSIA information can be obtained
at www.ICGtesting.com
Printed in the USA
261204LV00002B